BUCK ROGERS™

**adapted by
Carole and Robert Pierce**

**illustrated by
Joseph Forte**

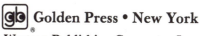 Golden Press • New York
Western Publishing Company, Inc.
Racine, Wisconsin

Five hundred years later, as the derelict spacecraft drifted back toward Earth, it was attacked by hostile skyfighters of the Draconian Dynasty. When the drifting ship failed to respond to their laser blasts, the Draconian pilots decided to take the odd craft back to their giant base ship.

Aboard the base ship *Draconia,* the astronaut was taken to the medical bay. There he drifted slowly into consciousness. A man was speaking: ". . . seems to have been frozen by space gases and perfectly preserved. He's fortunate that I, Kane, knew how to bring him back to life."

The astronaut groaned as he opened his eyes and blinked in the bright laboratory light. Dazedly he stared at the strange machinery and people around him. "Where am I?" he murmured.

"We will ask the questions," Kane replied rudely. "Who are you?"

"Captain Buck Rogers, United States Air Force."

A woman stepped forward. "Ah, yes, the United States," she said. "It used to be an

empire on the planet Earth centuries ago. Captain Rogers, you are aboard the star fortress *Draconia,* which is on a peace mission from the Draconian Dynasty to the Directorate of Earth. I am Princess Ardala, daughter of Draco, Conqueror of Space."

"Draconian Dynasty? Conqueror of Space?" muttered Buck Rogers. "What?"

Kane drew the Princess aside. "Say no more," he whispered. "This man may be a spy from Earth. We mustn't let him discover the real purpose of our mission. Why not send him back—with a micro-transmitter hidden on board his ship to show us the way through Earth's defense shield?"

"Very clever, Kane," Ardala replied. "Send him back at once. Tigerman," she snapped to her bodyguard, "remove him!"

To his surprise, Buck was put aboard his ship and launched toward Earth. He had just begun his reentry countdown when a squadron of sleek Starfighters roared up from Earth, surrounded him, and led him down into a shining domed city.

As he got out of his ship, a woman climbed down from the lead Starfighter and came toward him.

"Wow! This doesn't look like home!" Buck exclaimed. "Where are we, lady?"

"Colonel," the woman corrected. "I'm *Colonel* Wilma Deering, Commander of Earth's defense forces."

"Sorry, Colonel," Buck said. "You mean you're in charge of all this?"

"Yes," Colonel Deering said. "And you have violated our air space." Turning to a guard she ordered, "Arrest this trespasser and hold him for questioning."

The guards seized Buck, led him into a small white room, and left him. Buck began to pace impatiently around the room.

Suddenly a panel slid open and a man entered. "Hello, Captain Rogers," the man said. "I am Dr. Huer."

"Where am I and what is going on?" demanded Buck.

"All in good time, Captain Rogers," replied Dr. Huer. "Your questions will all be answered if you will just be patient."

The panel opened again and a small robot came in. "This is Twiki, your drone," said Dr. Huer, "and the computer box hanging from Twiki's neck is Dr. Theopolis, a member of our Council of Computers. Dr. Theopolis will brief you on your situation. I will leave you to get acquainted." Dr. Huer disappeared through the panel.

Twiki put the computer box on the table. It began to flicker. "You are Captain Buck Rogers," Dr. Theopolis said. "You left Earth in 1987 on a space mission."

"I know that part," Buck said impatiently. "Tell me what happened after that."

"Well, you have returned to Earth five hundred and four years later. You are now living in the twenty-fifth century."

"The twenty-fifth century?" gasped Buck. He was stunned. He stared at Dr. Theopolis and then at Twiki. His brain whirled with the immensity of it all.

Even after his briefing was over, Buck could scarcely believe he was in the twenty-fifth century. As he strolled with Wilma through a plaza in the Domed City, he said, "It's hard to think of this as Earth. It is so different from the Earth I knew."

"The great nuclear war destroyed everything you'd remember," Wilma said.

"What is outside the Domed City?"

"It's a horrible place we call Anarchia. Only criminals and mutants live there. The whole earth was so badly scorched in the war that nothing will grow, and we have to trade with other planets for food, water, and other supplies."

"Do you trade with the Draconians?"

"How did you know about them?" asked Wilma, surprised.

"I was taken aboard their ship. There I met a Princess Ardala, and she said something about a Draconian peace treaty with Earth. What's that all about?"

"The Draconians have conquered half the star system and need Earth as a base to conquer other galaxies. The peace treaty will give them landing privileges here in return for protection from space pirates who have been shooting down our supply ships."

"How do you know the Draconians won't try to conquer Earth?" asked Buck.

"We have their promise that their ships are unarmed."

"I'm not so sure they really are un-armed," said Buck. "Take me back to my spacecraft." In the hangar, he pointed to some fresh burn marks on the ship's fuse-lage. "If the Draconians are unarmed, and you didn't shoot at me, who did?" he said.

"Perhaps the pirates . . ."

"Pirates would have finished me off. I think the Draconian fighters must have fired on me before towing me aboard. If so, they are armed! If I were you I wouldn't let the Draconians inside Earth's defense shield until you have searched their ships for weapons. But of course it's none of my business," he added, heading for the exit.

"Where do you think you're going?" Wilma demanded.

"Outside the dome. I want to find out what happened to my family."

"That is strictly forbidden. You're still under arrest."

Buck kept walking. "You'll have to shoot me to stop me," he said.

Wilma drew her laser gun, then stopped. She just couldn't bring herself to shoot Buck. Glumly, she watched as he strode out of the hangar.

Buck, Dr. Theopolis, and Twiki passed through the gates of the glowing Domed City and crept cautiously into the twilight of Anarchia. They saw ruined buildings in streets overgrown with weeds, and shadowy semi-human mutant forms.

As Buck and his friends passed by, one of the mutants began to hammer on a lamppost with a piece of pipe. A horrible, deafening clanging arose as other mutants took up the signal. From every dim doorway and dark street corner, bands of the creatures formed and swarmed after the frightened trio.

Buck raced ahead of his friends and stumbled into a cemetery, sprawling over a headstone. He read, "EDNA AND JAMES ROGERS, THEIR SON FRANK AND DAUGHTER MARILYN." So his family *was* gone. He couldn't hold back his tears.

"We can't stay here, Buck," said Dr. Theopolis. "The mutants are coming!"

The dreadful mutant shapes surrounded Buck and his friends and began to close in on them. Suddenly, a harsh siren cut through the deafening clamor and bursts of laser fire cut down some of the mutants. At once the rest of the grunting mob scattered and scuttled away into the darkness.

An armed land cruiser screeched to a halt and Wilma stepped out. "Get in, Captain Rogers," she commanded.

"Not now," Buck replied. "I still have things to find out." He turned on his heel.

Wilma drew her laser gun, set it for stun, and aimed. "For the last time, halt," she ordered. A beam of light streaked from her gun, and Buck fell.

In the meantime, Wilma's guards had searched Buck's ship and found the hidden transmitter. At the next meeting of the Council of Computers, Earth's ruling body, Buck was brought to trial for spying.

Dr. Theopolis defended Buck stoutly. "I am programmed to know humans," he said, "and my sensors tell me that this man is good."

But it was to no avail. Dr. Apol, an unusually sinister-looking member of the Council, announced, "The state charges that Captain Rogers has revealed the safe corridor through our defense shield to our enemies. Captain Rogers can give us no proof that he was born on Earth and cannot explain why the alien transmitter was in his ship. I say he is a pirate spy—trying to prevent our treaty with the Draconians, and I say his life should be terminated."

Somehow, to Wilma, the sentence of life termination seemed so very harsh, and she could not get Buck out of her mind. Later, she remembered that Buck had claimed to have been on the *Draconia*. She went to Buck's prison cell and offered him a chance to prove his story by going with her to inspect the *Draconia*. Almost before Buck knew what was happening, he and Wilma had boarded a fleet of Starfighters and were on their way.

Buck was still new at piloting the sleek craft, but he was catching on fast. "Don't try any fancy tricks, Captain, just stay on Autoflight," Wilma warned him as she flew alongside his ship. "The pirates strike swiftly—too swiftly for human reactions. If the pirates attack, let your inboard defense computer take any necessary evasive action," she continued.

However, there was no sign of pirates, and Wilma's squadron soon started to enter one of the *Draconia's* landing bays.

In the control room of the *Draconia*, Kane watched the incoming Earth fleet on the scanner. "What are they up to?" he muttered to himself. "Oh, well, there is nothing incriminating that they can see."

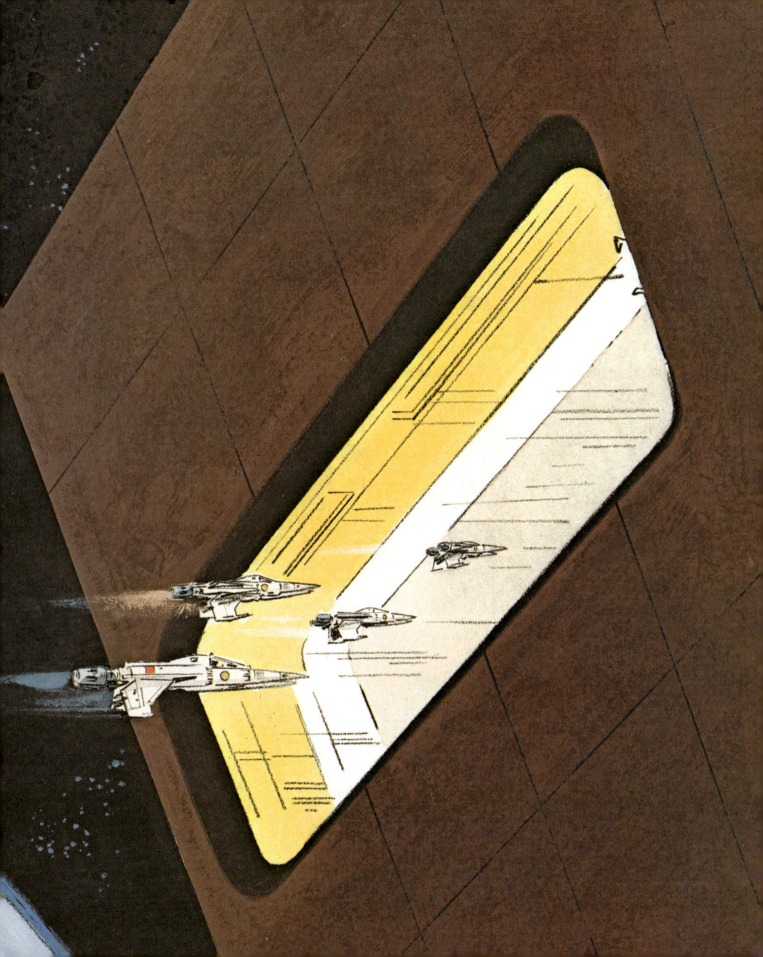

Kane, Ardala, and Tigerman met Wilma and Buck in the landing bay.

"Welcome aboard," Kane said, with an oily smile. "This is Princess Ardala, the daughter of the great Draco, Conqueror of Space."

"I am Colonel Deering," Wilma said. "And I believe you already know Captain Rogers."

Ardala regarded Buck coolly. "I haven't had the pleasure," she said.

"But of course you've met me!" Buck exclaimed in surprise. Wilma gave him a sharp look.

"Why are you here, Colonel Deering?" Kane demanded rudely.

"To escort the *Draconia* to Earth. The pirate forces are at their most dangerous in this sector."

The intercom suddenly crackled into life. "Hostile spacecraft approaching— ship under attack. Red alert! Red alert!"

Wilma, Buck, and the squadron pilots raced for their ships while the Draconians remained behind.

A fleet of pirate Marauders, evil-looking ships emblazoned with dragon's heads, swarmed around the *Draconia*. No sooner were the Starfighters airborne than the Marauders bore down upon them. Buck saw a Starfighter go into a violent roll. A Marauder rolled right after it and blew it out of the sky. Three more Starfighters were shot down in quick succession. Buck realized that Wilma's squadron was no match for the pirates, who seemed to know the Starfighters' maneuvers in advance.

Wilma's ship rocketed by with two pirate Marauders close behind, matching her wild gyrations move for move.

"Break right, Wilma!" Buck shouted. "Hit your retros!" He switched off his Autoflight, swung his ship into a steep turn, and blasted the pirate ships broadside. They exploded in flames.

The dogfight continued, with Buck finally wiping out the last of the Marauders. The two remaining Starfighters left the *Draconia* and limped back to Earth.

In the hangar, Buck inspected his Starfighter for damage.

"It's strange," he said to Wilma, "that the pirates were ready for every move our ships made. I think someone has given them the program for your Autoflight defense tactics. If I hadn't shut off my Autoflight we'd both be dead. You have a pirate spy in the Domed City, all right, but it isn't me."

That night, on Earth, a party was held in the Domed City to celebrate the peace treaty between Earth and the Draconian Dynasty.

When Dr. Theopolis and Twiki came by to get Buck for the party, Buck complained of a headache.

"Why didn't you tell us?" said Dr. Theopolis. "We'll get you a relaxant that will make you feel better. You go ahead."

Buck went into the glittering Hall of Mirrors. Crowds of people were strolling about the dance floor waiting for the party to begin. Dr. Theopolis and Twiki arrived and handed Buck the headache medicine just as Dr. Huer began to address the crowd. Buck slipped the bottle into his uniform sash.

"Citizens of the Inner City," Dr. Huer announced gravely, "at this historic moment a great spacecraft hovers over our heads. It comes not as an invader, but

completely unarmed—a symbol of peace and good will between Earth and the Draconian Dynasty. And here, as a representative from the Dynasty, is the Crown Princess Ardala! Let us welcome her."

There was a blast of music from silver trumpets and Ardala entered. "I salute the beginning of a glorious era of commerce and peace," she declared. "And, I have a special surprise for you—my father, the great Draco, has commanded the flagship *Draconia* to remain above your city, open to the public, as a permanent symbol of our good faith."

The crowd applauded as Kane escorted the Princess to the throne of honor.

"Little do these fools know," he whispered to her, "that at this very moment Draco is halfway here with his attack force. And thanks to our transmitter in Captain Rogers' ship, he will be able to find his way right through Earth's defense shield."

The orchestra began to play and the guests whirled about the dance floor in structured formations.

Buck danced with Ardala. "Well, Captain," she said, "are you enjoying your stay here on Earth?"

"Not really," said Buck. "They think I'm a spy."

"One of *my* spies?"

A plan was forming in Buck's mind. "They're not really sure," he said slyly. "By the way, how would I join your forces if I wanted to?"

"I will leave for the *Draconia* at midnight," Ardala whispered. "Join me on my private launch and we will discuss this."

Shortly after midnight, Ardala's private launch streaked away from the Domed City. Princess Ardala and Buck Rogers were aboard. Dr. Theopolis and Twiki, who had been ordered to follow Buck, were hiding in the galley.

Later, in her stateroom aboard the *Draconia,* Ardala told Buck her plans and tried to enlist his support. "You impress me, Captain," she said. "With your help I could not only conquer Earth, but also defeat my father and rule the Universe!"

Buck listened, stunned. At last he knew for sure that the Draconians intended to conquer Earth. He must find a way to warn his friends.

Suddenly he remembered the bottle of medicine that Dr. Theopolis and Twiki had given him for his headache. They had told him not to take more than one dose if he wanted to stay awake. Buck secretly put two doses of the medicine into Ardala's drink.

Soon after drinking the potion, Ardala was fast asleep.

Buck crossed the room and opened the door cautiously. Ardala's huge bodyguard, Tigerman, stood outside, his back to the door. Buck gently lifted Tigerman's laser gun from its holster. As Tigerman turned, Buck fired, and the huge mutant froze in his tracks. Buck carried him into Ardala's room, stepped outside, and locked the door. Then he dashed off down the corridor toward the *Draconia's* flight deck.

Twiki and Dr. Theopolis peered from a doorway as Buck ran by. "There he goes!" Dr. Theopolis exclaimed. "After him! If we lose him again, we'll be in trouble!"

Staying in the shadows, Buck crept out onto the flight deck and came upon a shocking sight. Draconian crewmen were busy arming fightercraft with missiles!

Then Buck saw that the fighters bore the dragon markings of the pirate Marauders. The pirate ships had really been disguised Draconian warships all along!

A Draconian soldier passed by. Buck pounced on him and dragged him into the shadows. Soon Buck emerged, wearing the soldier's uniform and helmet. He went straight to a missile storage bin. While the Draconians armed the forward tubes of each ship, Buck stole around to the rear and slipped missiles into the tailpipes.

At that very moment, Twiki and Dr. Theopolis arrived. "Look!" the doctor cried. "Armed warships! And Captain Rogers is wearing a Draconian uniform!"

Twiki sprang out in front of Buck and pointed a laser gun at him.

"Don't move, you traitor!" Dr. Theopolis hissed. "This gun isn't set to stun."

"Doc! Twiki! I'm not a traitor. Can't you see that the so-called pirate ships are disguised Draconian warships? The Draconians have been shooting down your supply ships to force you into the treaty with Draco. The treaty is only a trick to allow the Draconian forces to get close enough to Earth to attack you. I'm putting these torpedoes in the tailpipes of the pirate ships so they'll blow up in mid-air!"

"Of course! It's ingenious," Dr. Theopolis said, "if true—"

"You've got about ten seconds to decide it is true, unless you want to end up as scrap parts."

"All right, you win—but someone must get the news back to Earth. Twiki, take me to the Communications Room."

"Good luck," Buck called after them.

Meanwhile, in the royal apartments, Kane had unlocked Ardala's stateroom door and awakened her from her drugged sleep. Soon they realized that Buck must have discovered their attack preparations.

"He'll warn the people on Earth!" Ardala shouted. "We cannot wait for my father's forces to arrive. Give the order to attack at once!"

Two decks below, in the Communications Room, Twiki crept up to a console and stuck his metal hand into an electric panel. Sparks leapt out as the wiring short-circuited. The radio operator screamed, tore his headset off, and ran out of the room. Quickly Twiki held a microphone close to Dr. Theopolis and began to adjust the tuning dials on the console. The radio crackled as it warmed up.

"Earth Emergency Channel, come in please," whispered Dr. Theopolis.

Wilma's voice answered. "Emergency Channel Two. Colonel Deering on-line."

"This is Dr. Theopolis on board the *Draconia*. I followed Captain Rogers as ordered. The *Draconia* is armed and preparing to bomb the Domed City."

"So Buck Rogers *is* a traitor!"

"There is no time for me to explain now," said Dr. Theopolis. "You must launch all your fighters at once!"

On the flight deck of the *Draconia,* Kane had given the order to attack. In the launching area, Buck watched with an expectant smile as, one by one, the Draconian warships were catapulted out into the starry void and, one by one, they blew up in a brilliant orange ball of fire.

As Wilma and her squadron approached the *Draconia,* they were surprised to see the enemy ships exploding. Seizing their advantage, the Earth squadron pressed in to attack the mother ship with heavy fire.

Buck was still on the flight deck, watching a Draconian ship taxiing out to take off. Suddenly a voice on the intercom shouted, "Hold the launch! Our ships are blowing up!" The fighter stopped short. Buck started to run, but he was too late. A searing blast shattered the fighter, knocking Buck unconscious and pinning him down. Flames roared across the deck. Again the intercom blared. "Clear the area! Burning ship close to ammunition magazine!" Klaxons sounded. Sirens screamed.

With no fighters left and the landing bay aflame, the *Draconia* was helpless. Realizing that they were doomed, Kane and Ardala climbed into an emergency escape capsule and fired themselves out into space, hoping to be picked up by Draco. As they left, they bitterly blamed each other for the failure of their mission.

Streaking toward the *Draconia*, Wilma called urgently into her microphone, "The *Draconia* is ready to blow. Dr. Theopolis, I'm coming in to get you and Twiki."

"Forget us," Dr. Theopolis answered. "Find Buck."

"He is a traitor."

"You're wrong. He's the one who sabotaged the Draconian fighters and saved us."

"I'm coming in," Wilma repeated. "Find Buck Rogers and stand by."

Twiki scurried through the burning wreckage. Suddenly he heard a weak voice calling, "Twiki! I'm over here!"

Twiki rushed to Buck and tugged at the heavy beam pinning him down. "Don't worry, Captain," Dr. Theopolis said. "Wilma is on her way."

"She can't land!" Buck protested. "This ship is going to blow any second!"

Wilma was already taxiing up the deck. Twiki gave a mighty heave and Buck was free. Running through the smoke and flames to Wilma's ship, they scrambled aboard.

Wilma gunned her engines and the Star-fighter shot out of the launching bay. Just as they cleared the deck, the *Draconia* was wracked by a series of explosions that lit up the sky. Crammed in the Starfighter's tiny cockpit, Wilma, Buck, Dr. Theopolis, and Twiki headed for home.

Later, in the Domed City, the Council of Computers met again. Dr. Theopolis reported that he had discovered a direct transmission line from the sinister-looking computer, Dr. Apol, to the *Draconia*'s communications center. Dr. Apol had been sending secret information from Earth to Kane, so he was the real traitor. By unanimous vote, the Council condemned him to extinction.

"Let's not be hasty. I had no choice," argued Dr. Apol. "Kane twisted my circuits, corrupted my wiring. Have mercy, don't blow my . . ." Gray smoke began to curl up from his fuse panel and his voice groaned to a stop. His drone put his remains in a bucket and carried them out.

Once more there was a great celebration in the Hall of Mirrors. Earth was no longer threatened by pirates or overshadowed by the evil forces of Draco.

Buck Rogers knew that he could never return to his own time, but at least he was beginning to feel that he had earned a place in the new and bewildering world of the twenty-fifth century.